People Who Live in Antarctica

Debbie Croft

Contents

The Continent of Antarctica

The area of land around the South Pole is called Antarctica. It is the world's coldest and windiest continent. Antarctica is about twice the size of Australia and is covered in ice for almost the whole year.

Although it is very cold, Antarctica is a desert. Only a small amount of rain falls there each year.

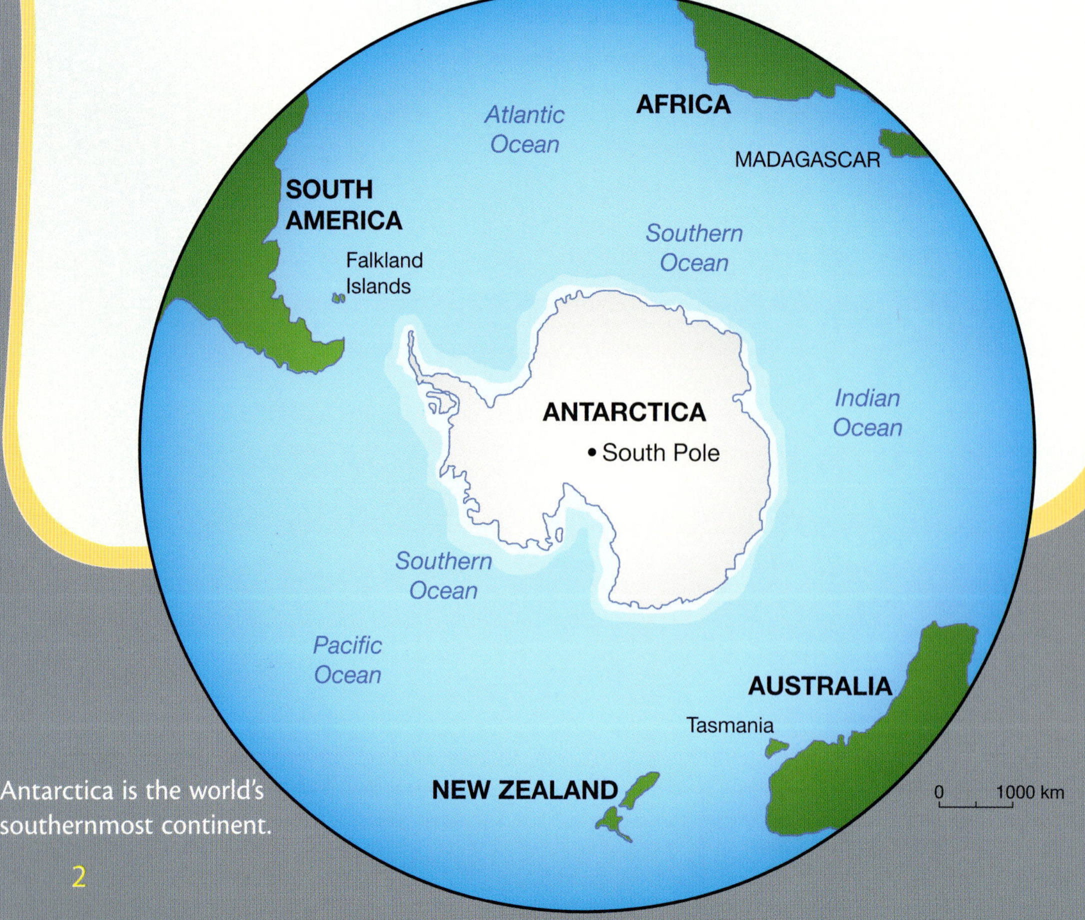

Antarctica is the world's southernmost continent.

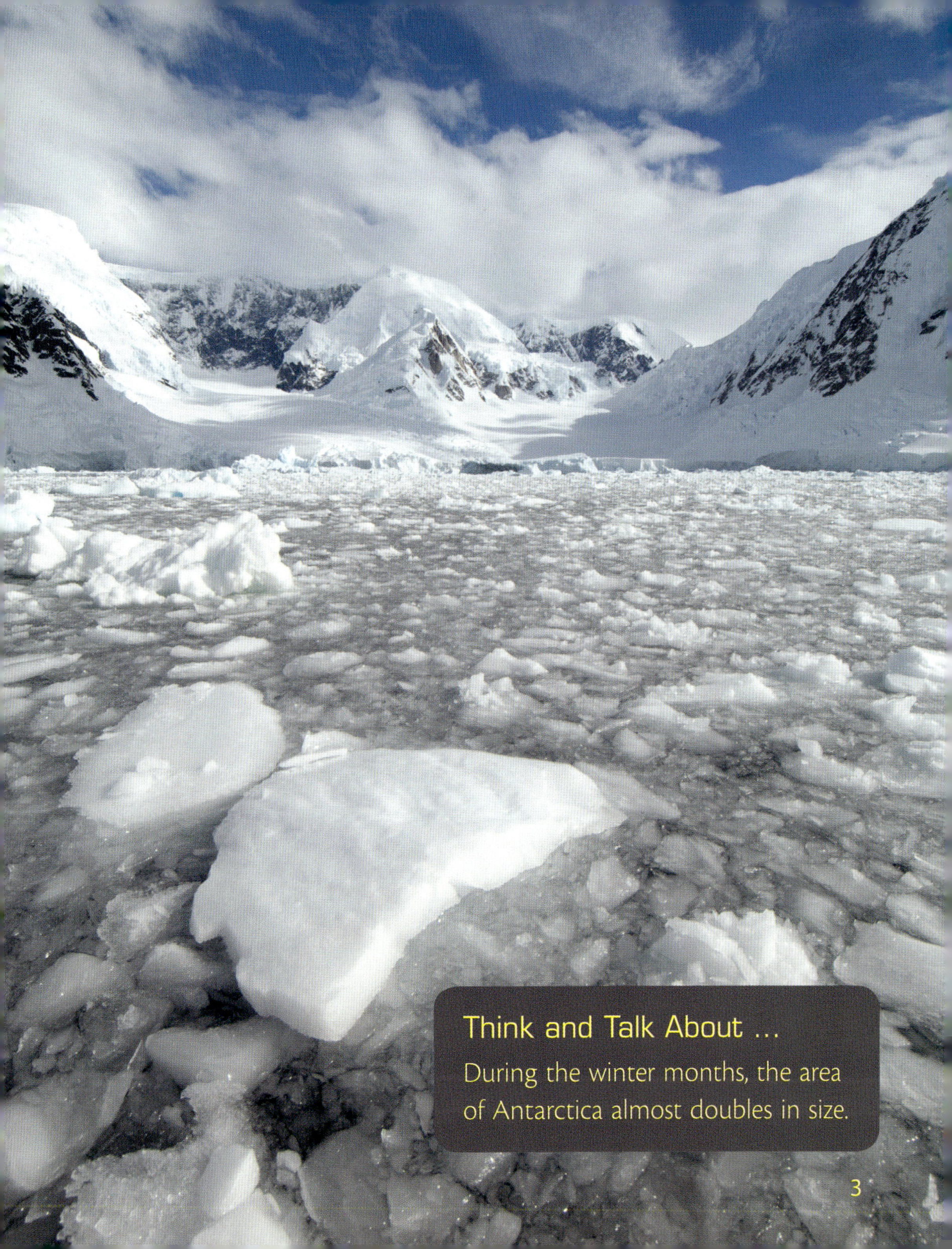

Think and Talk About ...

During the winter months, the area of Antarctica almost doubles in size.

People Who Work in Antarctica

During the winter, a few hundred people live and work in Antarctica. However, in the summer, about 5000 people from many different countries live and work there.

Scientists

Scientists from all around the world work at research stations in Antarctica. They study living **organisms**, the air and the environment.

Many scientists study how plants and animals **adapt** to the harsh conditions in Antarctica. They learn about the eating habits of **krill**, squid, fish, seabirds and mammals that live in the icy waters.

Some of the work that scientists do in this freezing environment cannot be done successfully anywhere else in the world. Antarctica is a **unique** place.

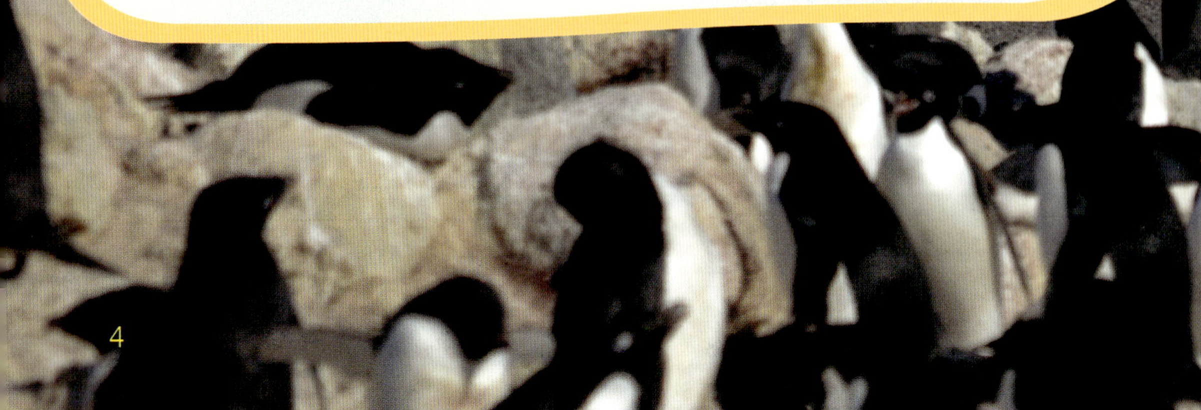

A scientist studies penguins in Antarctica.

Builders, Plumbers and Electricians

Builders, plumbers and electricians also work in Antarctica. These people put up new buildings at the research stations. They also maintain and repair older buildings where people live and work.

People who work in Antarctica often have to help shovel snow.

An electrician repairs the pipes at an Antarctic research station.

Electricians work inside an Antarctic research station.

Doctors

Doctors are very important in Antarctica. There is always at least one doctor on duty at each research station.

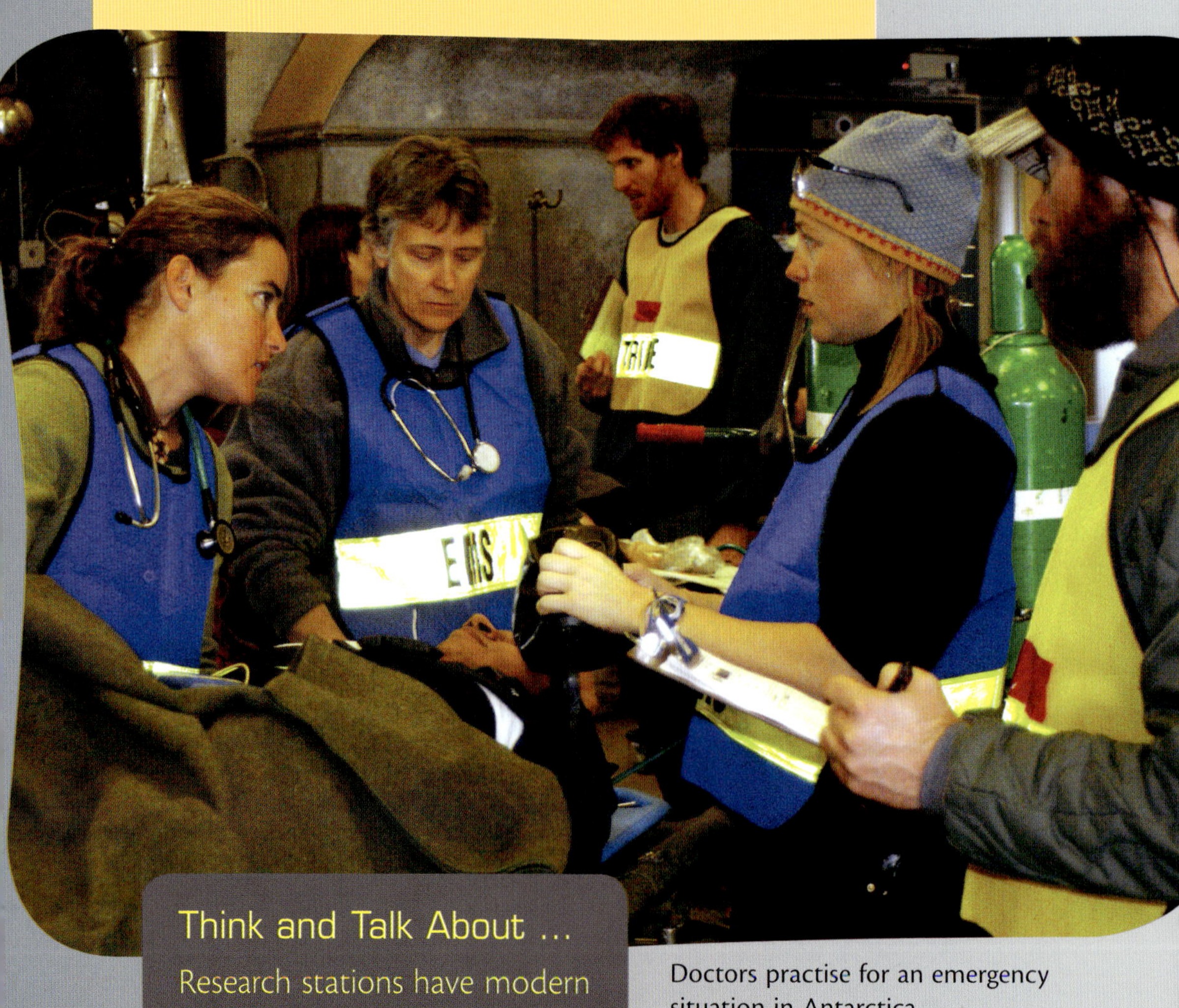

Doctors practise for an emergency situation in Antarctica.

Think and Talk About ...

Research stations have modern medical equipment.

Sometimes, doctors in Antarctica need to assist people who have had an accident.

The doctor at the research station **treats** people who become ill.
If people are injured while working,
or while doing other activities,
such as skiing or hiking,
they are able to receive medical help.

Living in Antarctica

Food

People living in Antarctica eat food that is similar to the food they would eat in their own homes. Each research station has a chef, who prepares healthy meals for the workers.

All the food that is needed must be delivered to the stations by ship during the summer months. In the winter, extra ice forms near the coast. This prevents ships from **anchoring** close to the research stations.

Fresh fruit and vegetables are only **available** for a short time after supplies have been delivered. When these supplies are used up, people eat foods that have been tinned or frozen.

Think and Talk About ...

At some research stations, tomatoes and lettuce are grown in special buildings called "hot houses".

The chef at an Antarctic research station makes a dessert for the workers to enjoy.

Shelter

In Antarctica, people live in modern buildings. All the rooms are heated, so everyone stays warm and comfortable indoors.

Bedrooms in Antarctic research stations are small, but warm and comfortable.

To learn about Antarctica, scientists often need to live away from the research stations. During this time, they stay in different types of shelters. Sometimes, they sleep in huts or tents. Many of these can be moved from place to place. If the workers are outdoors for a long time, they live in special vans that are more secure than a hut or tent.

Scientists sometimes stay in tents when they are working away from the research station.

Water

Snow is heated in large tanks so people have water for drinking and showering.

Everyone is reminded to use only as much water as they need, and not to waste it.

Workers pour snow into a tank that melts it to make water that is suitable to drink.

Staying Warm Outside

People who work outdoors in Antarctica wear special clothing to stay warm and dry.
Wind jackets are often worn over other layers of clothes.

If people get too warm when they are working, they can open the zippers or flaps in their jacket to let cold air inside.
Sometimes, they remove their jacket, or take off one or more layers of clothing underneath it.

People who work outdoors in Antarctica need to wear suitable clothing.

Think and Talk About ...

It is important that people who work outdoors do not become overheated.

Leisure

Living in Antarctica can be very enjoyable. Sometimes, people hike or ski over the ice and sleep in huts away from the stations.

Other people enjoy taking photographs of the beautiful **scenery** and watching the amazing wildlife.

People who live in Antarctica often take part in outdoor activities when they are not working.

Think and Talk About ...

Whales can be seen breaching, or leaping out of the water, off the coast of Antarctica.

If the weather outdoors is too windy or cold,
people play indoor games,
such as volleyball or basketball.

Others just relax and watch television,
listen to music or read a book.
People can also keep in contact
with their families using computers.

Think and Talk About ...

Scientists in Antarctica live and work for several months with the same group of people.

A Team Effort

The **incredible** work of the scientists in Antarctica is shared with people throughout the world.

However, this work would not be possible without the **assistance** of many other people, including builders, chefs and doctors.

A chef prepares a meal for workers at a research station.

Scientists discuss their research in Antarctica.

Dr Walker's Blog

I have spent my first week working in a research station in Antarctica, and it's such a great experience!

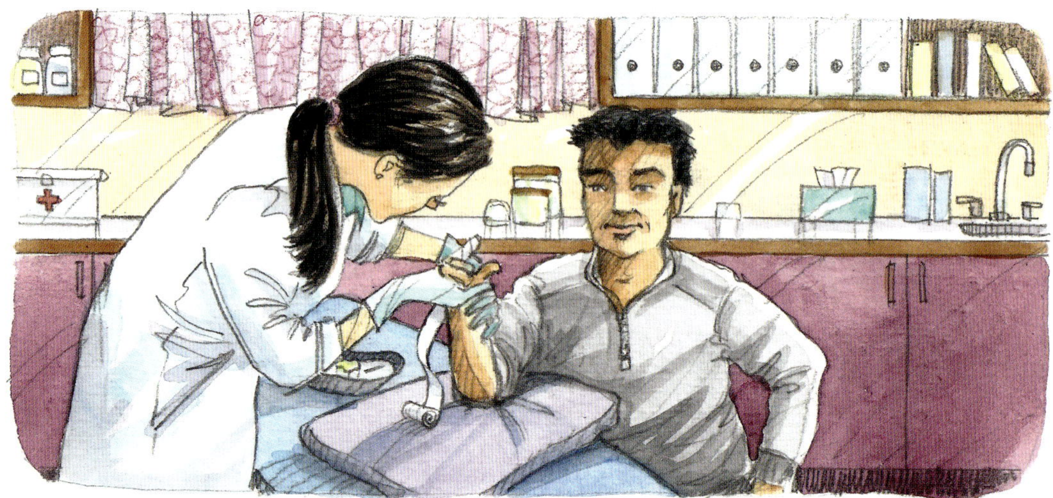

This morning began like most other days – with medical work. A builder had cut his finger and I decided it needed stitching. I cleaned the wound, stitched it closed and wrapped it with a small, clean bandage. I knew he would want to continue working.

Then, I did some dental work for one of the scientists. I had to replace a filling that had fallen out of her tooth. We were both very pleased I had learnt some basic dental procedures before I left home.

After that, I spent some time checking the medical equipment and making sure there were enough supplies in the clinic. I felt relieved knowing everything was well organised, and I was prepared if an emergency arose.

Later this afternoon, I sorted the research station's mail. Stamp collectors from all around the world send stamped, self-addressed envelopes to the station here in Antarctica.

They think it is fantastic to have an Antarctic postmark on their postage stamp when the letter arrives in their mailbox! This makes their stamp much more valuable.

In my spare time, I've been helping a group of scientists. On some days, there is no medical work to be done, which is a good sign.

Last Friday, I went on a field trip with the scientists to count penguin chicks. I didn't go too far away from the research station, so I could return quickly if I was needed.

Then, at the weekend, I had an opportunity to do some cross-country skiing. It was hard work, but it was so much fun, too. It reminded me of when I went skiing last year on our family holiday.

I've had dinner now, and the chef made another delicious meal for all the workers on the station.

Tonight we enjoyed a beef stew with vegetables – it was almost as good as the one I make at home!

Next weekend, if the weather is suitable, a group of us is going ice climbing. I'm really looking forward to that, as it will be a new experience for me.

I'll let you know how it goes!

Dr Lauren Walker

Glossary

adapt (*verb*)	to adjust to different conditions
anchoring (*verb*)	fastening securely
assistance (*noun*)	help or aid
available (*adjective*)	able to be used
incredible (*adjective*)	unbelievable or marvellous
krill (*noun*)	a small animal with a shell that lives in the sea
organisms (*noun*)	living things, such as animals or plants
scenery (*noun*)	natural features of a landscape
treats (*verb*)	cures or heals
unique (*adjective*)	being the only one of a type

Index